THAT MONSTER ON THE BLOCK

BY SUE GANZ-SCHMITT • ILLUSTRATED BY LUKE FLOWERS

two lions

To Martin, Jensen, and India—forever my favorites on the block!
With gratitude to Sharon Darrow, VCFA, and Jennifer Unter
—S. G-S.

For my monstrously talented pal, Joey Ellis
(and his sidekick, Wolfie Monster).
Thanks for accepting me for the clown I am
and for giving me a warm welcome
into your neighborhood of creativity and inspiration.
—L. F.

Published by Two Lions, New York

www.apub.com

Amazon, the Amazon logo, and Two Lions are trademarks of Amazon.com, Inc., or its affiliates.

ISBN-13: 9781542005333 (hardcover)
ISBN-10: 1542005337 (hardcover)

The illustrations are rendered in digital media.

Book design by Tanya Ross-Hughes
Printed in China

First Edition
10 9 8 7 6 5 4 3 2 1

Somebody was moving into Vampire's old house today. The house was dark and dreary. One of Monster's favorites on the block.

Maybe the new neighbor would be an ogre, and Monster would be invited to swim in his mucky, murky swamp!

Or a greedy goblin with piles of gold to jump into— right up to Monster's snout!

No, wait! Maybe it would be a dastardly dragon. Monster loved a good, greasy barbecue.

Inside, Monster worked on his welcome growl.

GRRRREETINGS! GRRREAT TO MEET YOU!

He peered at the polka-dotted van.
The movers took out a trampoline,
toted trunks, and unloaded a unicycle.

Then . . .

. . . a clown?

A CLOWN!

And that clown was cartwheeling
across the yard.

Monster picked up the phone
and called Zombie.

BEEP BEEP
BOOP BEEP

"Our new neighbor is
**a cartwheeling
clown!**"
said Monster.

*"Unnnnnhhh,
unnnnnhhh,
unnnnnhhh,"*
said Zombie.

"Just what I thought too,"
said Monster. "There goes
the neighborhood!"

BOOP BOOP
BEEP BEEP

"There is a **clown** living
among us," said Monster.

"*Aaaaaahhhh,
aaaaaahhhh!*"
said Mummy.

"Yes," said Monster.
"Before you know it
there will be more!"

BEEP BOOP
BEEP BEEP

"Did you see that **clown?**
Right on our block!"
said Monster.

"*Raawrrrrgghh!*"
said Yeti.

"I agree one hundred percent.
Clowns are creepy," said Monster.

Monster did not welcome Clown
to the neighborhood.
Nobody did.
So Clown went around
to introduce himself.

Clank-Clank

DinG-DonG

KnocK-KnocK

"*YOO-HOO!*" Clown called.
Monster did not answer.
Neither did the neighbors.

Clown left notes along with surprises.

Do come by and CLOWN AROUND! —Your NEW neighbor AND friend, CLOWN

Monster got a can of delightful worms.

Zombie got a delicious cake.

Yeti got a bouquet of flowers.

And Mummy got a . . .

Clown sat on his porch.
He sat and waited. And waited and sat.
No one came around.

But Clown couldn't stay down for long.

He put on a happy tune, gave his house a makeover, and popped up a tent.

Monster called a neighborhood meeting.
"This is out of control!"

And so was the meeting.

"I will scare him away!" Monster declared.

So at midnight, Monster made a terrible clatter,
played his spookiest music, and let out a mighty

ROAR!

(He even scared
himself a little.)

But Clown did not hear any of it. He was out.

Zombie's two-headed cat was stuck
in a tree. Clown got him down.

Yeti lost one of her dancing shoes,
so Clown brought her a new pair.
They fit perfectly.

And when Mummy's sheets flew away, Clown brought them back.

The next day, circus music woke Monster from a wonderfully awful nightmare.

Monster called the neighbors for another meeting.
But nobody answered.
"It's time for me to have a word with that bozo!"

STOMP
STOMP
STOMP

CIRCUS
SCHOOL
NOW OPEN!

WELCOME NEIGHBOR!

Doot-doot-dootle
Dootle-oot
Doot-dootle

That music . . .
it was quite catchy!

SNARL
SNARL
SNARL

POPOBOT

A warm, buttery smell
made Monster drool.

GROWL
GROWL
GROWL

"Welcome!" greeted Clown.
"You're just in time for
cartwheeling class!"

WELCOME
★ TO ★
CIRCUS
SCHOOL

"Raawrrrrgghh!" hollered Yeti.

"He's fun for the neighborhood?"
said Monster.

"You're ALL hanging around
with this clown?!"

"*Unnnnnhhh,*" shouted Zombie.

"And zero percent creepy?" said Monster.

"*Aaaaaahhhh!*" waved Mummy.

"Oh, **floggerbogger!**" said Monster. "Fine! I'll unwind a bit and give him a chance."

Clown helped Monster take on the trapeze, ride the unicycle,
and master the cartwheel—until the sun settled down.

That Clown! He was more fun than a barrel of popcorn!

The next day, Monster called Clown.

BeeP BeeP
BeeP BeeP

"Could you join us Sunday for sludgeberry swirl scones and tea?" asked Monster.
"Yes! I'm sure I can juggle it!" said Clown.

That Sunday as Monster poured the tea,
a moving van pulled onto the block.

"Another new neighbor?" grumbled Monster.

Out popped . . .

. . . a unicorn.

"A rainbow-loving, magical unicorn?"
Monster growled.

"UNICORNS!"

He turned to his neighbors.

"Do they eat scones?"
asked Monster.